TECHNICAL
FOUL

TECHNICAL FOUL

RICH WALLACE

SCHOLASTIC INC.
New York Toronto London Auckland Sydney
Mexico City New Delhi Hong Kong Buenos Aires

ISBN 0-439-79972-4

12 11 10 9 8 7 6 5 4 3   6 7 8 9 10 11/0

Printed in the U.S.A.   40

First Scholastic printing, January 2006

Book design by Jim Hoover
Set in Caslon 224 Book

For Cameron

· CONTENTS ·

1. GAME ON THE LINE — 1

2. THE GO-TO GUY — 8

3. NO HEROES — 13

4. A CHEAP SHOT? — 18

5. EMOTIONALLY DRAINED — 28

6. BLACK, WHITE, PURPLE, OR GREEN — 34

7. A LOT TO PROVE — 39

8. TEAM CHEMISTRY — 49

9. GET ME THE BALL — 57

10. TAKING A BREAK — 70

11. OUT OF THEIR GAME — 75

12. A NIGHT OUT — 82

13. PLAYOFF PRESSURE — 90

14. THE NIGHT BEFORE — 94

15. ALL OR NOTHING — 97

Game on the Line

*T*he ball came to Jared near the basket, with a defender guarding him tightly. Jared made a quick half turn to his right, then pivoted left and dribbled, driving to the hoop. His shot hit softly off the backboard and into the basket.

"About time," said Spencer Lewis, the point guard.

Jared ignored the comment. Less than a minute remained, and Hudson City trailed by two points. "Tough defense now!" Jared shouted as they retreated. "We need a stop!"

Hudson City had led for most of the game, but

the team's shooting had gone cold in the fourth quarter. Specifically, it was Jared who'd turned to ice. He'd missed four straight shots before that last basket, and Spencer had griped after every one. In the meantime, Memorial had rallied, taking its first lead of the game.

Memorial called for a time-out with about thirty seconds left to play. Jared wiped his face on his red jersey as he and the other Hudson City players jogged to the bench.

Coach Davis cleared his throat and looked at Spencer, who nodded. "We have to get the ball back," Coach said. "Foul if you need to, but let's get a steal if we can. Take the best shot available."

Jared looked up at the bleachers in the small Hudson City Middle School gym. About fifty students were watching the late-afternoon game.

Memorial passed the ball in, and the point guard dribbled to the top of the key. They could run out the clock and win the game without taking a shot. Hudson City had to get the ball.

"Pressure!" Jared shouted.

Spencer and Fiorelli hounded the Memorial

guard and forced him to stop dribbling. The guard held the ball away from the defenders and frantically looked for someone to pass to. He sent a quick bounce pass into the paint, but Jared stepped in front of his man and intercepted it.

Time was running out. Jared dribbled quickly up the court and straight toward the basket. Spencer was on his right, calling for the ball, but Jared was going all the way with this one.

Jared drove into the lane with a pair of Memorial players at his sides. He could hear the spectators counting down the seconds: "Six-five-four . . ."

"Trailing!" That was Jason Fiorelli, wide open at the free-throw line.

Jared stopped his dribble and launched a fade-away jump shot from six feet, leaning slightly toward the end line to avoid a defender's outstretched hand.

The ball bonked off the rim and fell to the floor. A Memorial player grabbed it and held it tight as the buzzer sounded, ending the game.

Hudson City had lost, 54–52.

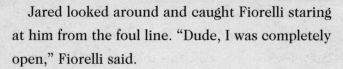

Jared looked around and caught Fiorelli staring at him from the foul line. "Dude, I was completely open," Fiorelli said.

"Ball hog!" That was Spencer.

The opposing players shook hands and walked off the court. Jared took a last glance at the scoreboard. Another loss. They'd had such high hopes at the start of the season, but now they were 0–3.

I'm not getting much support out there, Jared thought. He'd been the high scorer in all three games, but the result had been three tough losses.

The team was quiet in the locker room, showering and dressing and then sitting in front of their lockers to wait for the coach. Jared took out his comb and ran it through his wavy brown hair.

Coach Davis wasn't happy when he finally came in.

Mr. Davis was just one year out of college, and he was much quieter than last year's coach. He was the shyest coach Jared had ever had. And the most nervous. His armpits were wet with sweat.

"For some reason we can't seem to hold on to a lead," Coach said, stammering a little. "We've had a second-half lead in every game we've played, and every time we've blown it. Anybody have an answer for that?"

The players just looked around. Jared caught Spencer's eyes and they glared at each other. The two were supposed to be the leaders of this team. Both had been starters last year as fifth graders. Now, as the veterans of the team, they had big expectations. The two captains: Spencer, short and black; Jared, tall and white.

"Well," said the coach when no one spoke up. "We'll be running in practice tomorrow, I can tell you that. If we're running out of gas in the fourth quarter, there's a definite way to overcome that. It's called effort."

They left the gymnasium and stepped out into the cool, early evening air. Jared began walking across the blacktop play area toward the street, but he stopped when he heard footsteps behind him. He was surprised to see Spencer, who lived in the opposite direction.

"What's up, Spence?" Jared said, looking down into his shorter teammate's large brown eyes.

"You blew it, Jared."

Jared shook his head. "Hey. I had twenty-two points, pal."

"You took twenty-eight shots!" Spencer said. "That's more than the rest of the team combined. Do the math. The rest of us scored thirty."

Jared bit down on his lip. He and Spencer weren't close, but they'd never been hostile, either. Spencer looked tough with his close-cropped dark hair and muscular arms. Was this guy looking for a fight?

Jared thought for a few seconds, then said, "I'm the go-to guy, Spence. The man in the clutch."

"You won't be much longer if you keep forcing shots," Spencer said. "Just watch how often the pass *won't* come your way if you never pass it back."

They stared across at each other again. "Coach'll bench you if you don't feed me the ball," Jared said.

"Coach isn't exactly a basketball genius," Spencer answered. "We're in shape. We're just not a team. On that last play you had two wide-open options—me and Fiorelli. You forced a lame-butt shot because that's all you know how to do. If you make a simple pass, we tie that game. Instead you have to try to be a hero."

Jared swallowed hard and blinked. He knew he should have made the shot. Spencer and Fiorelli would have probably missed it, too.

"Twenty points a game," Jared said, tapping himself on the chest.

"Yeah? And your shooting percentage is practically single digits," Spencer said. "Just think about it, all right? You're a good player, but you're not helping the team. At least not as much as you think you are."

Spencer walked away. Jared watched him go.

What did Spencer know, anyway? Spencer'd had his share of turnovers and missed shots today. He'd made plenty of bad passes and got burned on defense a few times. He was just as much to blame for the loss, Jared decided.

Besides, he thought, *without my twenty-two points, we wouldn't even have been close.*

The Go-To Guy

Jared couldn't sit still at dinner, thinking about the last shot that he'd missed. "I've made shots like that a million times," he told his dad. "I never miss it in the driveway."

"There aren't any defenders in the driveway, Jag," Mr. Owen said with a laugh. "It's a long season, Jared. You guys will start winning."

"We'd better," Jared said. "We won't even make the playoffs if we don't get hot soon."

Jared's mom was working the evening shift at the hospital, so he and his dad were eating tuna-fish sandwiches and pasta at the kitchen table.

"I'll try to get to one of your games in the next week or so," Dad said. "I think I can cut out of work early next Thursday."

"Sounds good," Jared said. He set down his fork and pushed away his empty plate.

"You want more pasta?" Dad asked. "There's plenty."

"No thanks," Jared said. "I think I'll go out and shoot."

"It's getting pretty cold out there."

"I don't care."

"You ought to digest your dinner for a little while," Dad said. "Otherwise it'll come back up."

Jared shrugged. "I'm just going to shoot, not run. My touch was way off today. I don't know why. I just couldn't make a shot when it mattered."

Jared went up to his room to get his basketball. He pulled on a New Jersey Devils sweatshirt and glanced at the photos on his dresser—team pictures from junior football and Little League, and one from his guitar recital the previous spring. He also had a couple of bowling trophies, and medals from a local track meet where he'd won the long jump and the 200-meter dash. He'd had success in every sport he'd tried.

Jared stepped out to the narrow driveway and began dribbling slowly, working the ball from hand to hand. There was no light to turn on, but the streetlight around the corner kept the night from getting completely dark, so he could always see the basket. And the light from his kitchen and the house next door also made it brighter.

The old houses in this neighborhood were tightly packed, with only about two feet of space between the driveway and the walls of the homes. That's one reason why Jared was a great shooter from close to the basket: in the driveway, he couldn't get any farther away unless he went straight back to the street.

He tossed up a jumper that swished through the net, then raced in and grabbed the ball, softly banking it in off the small backboard, which was attached to a pole.

Jared loved to hear the *bonk, bonk, bonk* of the ball off the cement driveway and to watch the gentle flight of a shot. It seemed so easy here, as if he could do no wrong. He had spent countless hours at this basket over the past couple of years, driving past imaginary defenders and tossing in game-winning shots.

All of those solitary practice sessions had paid off—he was the best player in the school. But one thing he hadn't learned in all those hours alone was when to pass the ball. He wasn't much of a teammate.

Spencer was probably right. There were times when Jared could help the team more by giving up the ball than by shooting it. He'd work on it. But when the game was on the line, he knew he was the man to take over.

The go-to guy, he told himself. *You have to be that man.*

Jared looked over at the house next door and waved to old Mr. Murphy, who was watching from his kitchen. He trotted out to the sidewalk, then shifted low and sprinted up the driveway, dribbling past one defender after another.

The clock was ticking down, and another

player was in Jared's face. He stopped short, fading back and lofting the ball high over the imaginary defender's outstretched hands. The ball hit the backboard at just the right angle and dropped through the hoop.

Game winner!

Jared raised his arms in the dark and smiled. He never missed that shot—the short fade-away jumper in the final seconds of a game. That shot was a lock. It was golden.

At least out here in the driveway it was. Jared stared at the backboard for a few seconds, right at that sweet spot where the ball would hit before settling safely into the basket.

He hadn't hit that spot this afternoon. With the game on the line, he'd blown it.

No Heroes

Mr. Vega, the math teacher, was writing on the blackboard, so Jared turned around and whispered to Jason Fiorelli, "Think we'll be running all afternoon?"

"Depends," said Fiorelli. He played forward and was nearly as tall as Jared and definitely more agile. He had a presence that exuded confidence. "Davis gets bored pretty quickly when we do drills. He'd rather watch us scrimmage. He'll probably start off real tough, then decide we learned our lesson."

"Yeah. That's not the problem, anyway. We're in

good shape. Just not smart."

Fiorelli nodded. "We play stupid sometimes. I mean we should be 3 and 0, not the opposite."

"No question," Jared said.

"Jared." That was Mr. Vega.

"Yes, sir?"

"Eyes front please."

"No problem."

"Unless Mr. Fiorelli has something more interesting to say than I do."

Several students giggled. Jared shook his head. "How could Fiorelli possibly have something more interesting than *math* to talk about?"

Mr. Vega raised his eyebrows and gave a small smile.

"We *were* talking about math," Fiorelli said. "I was saying to Jared how the inverse of three and zero is zero and three. And he said he wanted to get smarter. Really. He did."

Mr. Vega nodded and smiled a little more broadly. "Thank you, Jason. You'll both get smarter by looking at this equation on the blackboard."

"No problem," Fiorelli said. "I'm with you."

•••

Practice started with ten laps around the gymnasium, then a series of sprinting drills. Coach Davis had the players sit in the bleachers after that. He stressed that the running wasn't a punishment for losing, simply a matter of conditioning. "Somehow we fall apart late in the game, and the only factor I can think of is that we're just getting too tired to execute." Coach looked right at Spencer, as he always seemed to do when he needed to make a coaching decision.

"It's not that," said Spencer, who had taken a seat on the bottom row of the bleachers. He was holding a basketball between his knees. "Some of us just panic when the score gets tight and think we have to do it all ourselves." He turned and glanced at Jared, then looked back at the coach. "Some of us think we have to turn into heroes."

"And are you one of them?" Coach asked.

"Nope."

"So you're blaming your teammates?"

"I'm just saying what it is," Spencer said. "Jared here thinks he doesn't have to pass the ball. He takes lousy shots over and over when the rest of us are open."

Coach looked up at Jared. Jared just shrugged. He knew that Coach Davis had little coaching experience. The previous coach had resigned last spring, and Davis hadn't been assigned the job until late October. He'd even told the players at the first practice session that he'd never coached a team before. "But I know the game," he'd said. "I'm a fan."

Jared wiped his mouth with the sleeve of his gray T-shirt, which was damp with sweat. "I shoot because that's what I do best," Jared said. "I'm the leading scorer. Scorers have to shoot."

"And shooters have to pass," Spencer snapped. "At least some of the time they do."

"Spencer's right," said Fiorelli, "but it isn't all Jared's fault, either. We're good players. We're just not playing like a team. We're thinking too much about how many points we all score. What matters is scoring more than the other team."

"Hey, speak for yourself," Spencer said. "I'm not the guy with all of my individual stats memorized. The only stat I care about is our record. And our record stinks."

Coach Davis held up his hand. "I don't care what the record is. What I care about is playing hard, playing smart, and acting like a team. If we've got some rivalries boiling up here that I didn't know about, then it's time to iron them out."

Spencer bounced the basketball and stood up. "Can we play some ball now, Coach? Seems to me we can fix things better by hammering them out on the court. We could talk all night or we could start getting better. We've got another game tomorrow. I say we play some ball."

Coach looked at Spencer, then at Fiorelli, and then at Jared. "All right," he said with a shrug. "I guess we should play some ball."

A Cheap Shot?

On his way to the cafeteria for lunch the next day, Jared stopped by his locker. As he rooted around in the locker looking for a pen, he felt a smack on his arm.

Jason Fiorelli was grinning at him as he turned.

"What's up?" Jared said.

"Just checking on ya," Fiorelli said. "My man Spencer's been giving you grief."

"He's talking too much," Jared said. "If he doesn't watch out, he's gonna get it. Yeah, I made some mistakes, but like he hasn't? I don't think so. He'd better quit whining."

"He's just trying to keep things in balance," Fiorelli said. "He's the point guard, the *man*. He's running the show."

"He's running it bad," Jared said. "If he wants to talk, he should be positive out there. The whole fourth quarter he was riding my butt. Every time I missed a shot, I had to listen to him gripe."

"He's just trying to make us win, dude."

"What he's doing is making us lose."

Jared slammed his locker shut and shook his head. "I'm getting tired of his mouth. We'd better win this afternoon. I'm even more tired of losing."

Jared raised his arm and shouted for the basketball, leaning into the defender who was guarding him. Jared was tired after nearly three hard quarters of basketball, but he had a lot of fight in him. He had good position near the basket, but Spencer was still dribbling, scanning the court. "Feed it here!" Jared yelled.

Instead, Spencer passed the ball to Ryan Grimes, who drove toward the basket. Jared stepped out to set a screen for his teammate. Ryan

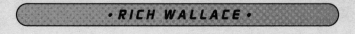

came hard and his defender smacked into Jared. The whistle blew.

The action stopped and Jared stepped toward the free-throw line, certain that he'd been fouled. But the referee was pointing toward him. "Foul on number thirty-three, red," he said.

Jared's mouth fell open and he stared at the official. "I had position," he said.

"But you were moving your feet," the official said. "The foul's on you."

Jared shook his head as he looked up at the scoreboard. Hudson City was trailing by four points. "Get me the ball," he said sharply to Spencer.

"Make some shots," Spencer replied.

Jared could feel his frustration mounting. He'd missed three straight shots, and now Spencer was freezing him out.

Emerson added to its lead with a quick layup, and Hudson City took possession.

Fiorelli had the ball in the corner, and he fired up a long jumper. Jared and the Emerson center went shoulder to shoulder, pushing for the ball as it bounded off the rim. Jared grabbed it and went right back up to shoot, but the Emerson player shoved hard and Jared missed the shot.

"Where's the foul?" Jared shouted to the referee as the players ran back up the court.

"No foul," said the official.

"You're blind!" Jared said. "Get some glasses."

The referee blew his whistle. "That's a *T*," he said, putting his hands together to make a T shape, signaling a technical foul. "Number thirty-three, red."

Jared shook his head and let out his breath.

"Nice going," said Spencer sarcastically as he walked over.

"Back off," Jared said.

"You're really helping us today," Spencer said. "Can't shoot and can't keep your mouth shut."

Jared thrust his arm quickly toward Spencer, smacking his shoulder and sending his teammate back a couple of steps. Spencer squared up to fight, and Fiorelli got between the two players. "Calm down," he said. "This ain't the place for that."

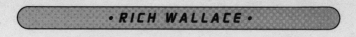
The official blew his whistle again, pointed toward Jared, and said, "You're gone! Hit the bench." He walked to the scorer's table and said, "Number thirty-three is ejected."

Jared walked quickly to the end of the Hudson City bench and sat down hard, staring at the floor and exhaling in a huff. *Bunch of jerks*, he thought. *I barely touched the guy.*

Coach Davis was glaring at the floor. He turned toward Jared and said, "Hey."

Jared raised his head and looked over.

"You can't lose your cool like that," Coach said.

Jared frowned and looked back at the game. Spencer gave him a little smirk as he brought the ball up the floor. Jared was seething—if Spencer had kept his mouth shut, everything would have been all right. *I'm no hot head,* he thought. *It's Spencer's fault for goading me on.*

But with Jared on the bench, the Hornets began to play more like a team. The ball moved from player to player, and they found openings in the defense. Little by little they ate away at the margin, finally taking the lead midway through the fourth quarter. From there, Spencer and Fiorelli took control, and Hudson City had its first win of the season.

Jared's hair was damp from the shower as he left the locker room, and the cold air bit at his ears. He needed to get home, to put this game behind him. They'd finally won one, but he felt worse than he had after the losses.

Spencer's voice, sounding high-pitched and mocking, stopped him as he reached the chain-link fence. "Oh, Jared!"

Jared stopped and walked back toward Spencer and Fiorelli, who were halfway across the blacktop area. "What do you want?" he asked gruffly.

"You think this is over?" Spencer said. "Not quite, my friend. I don't let cheap shots like that one go by unrewarded."

"Cheap but justified," Jared said sharply.

"Jared—we're *teammates,* jerk. At least the rest of us are. You almost cost us another ball game.

Thank God you got thrown out."

Jared sneered. "Fifteen points, nine rebounds."

"I know the statistics," Spencer said. "Look at the record. We finally won a game because you spent the last quarter on the bench."

Fiorelli was standing back with his arms crossed. Willie Shaw and a couple of other players had come over, too.

Spencer pointed at Jared. "You smack your own teammate right on the court," he said. "What a jerk. . . . I don't let things like that just slide, buddy. You going to the high school game tonight?"

"I might."

"Yeah? Well, maybe I'll see you there. . . . Like outside, by the tennis courts." Spencer spread his fingers and brought them together in a fist.

Jared squared his shoulders. "Why wait till then?"

"You wanna fight now?"

"Your choice, pal." Jared spit off to the side and looked back.

Fiorelli spoke up. "Not here. They'll kick your

butts off the team if you get caught."

"There's places we can go."

"Yeah," Spencer said. "I know a few where you can."

"Big talk for a short man."

"Short and strong."

They eyed each other for a few seconds. Jared swallowed hard, but then he took a step toward Spencer. Spencer glared back and put up his hands. Jared reached out to Spencer's chest and gave a one-handed shove.

Spencer whacked Jared's arm away and went into a defensive stance. "Come on," he said. "Let's go."

"I'm ready." But Jared didn't want to fight, and he suspected that Spencer didn't either. "I'll fight you," he said. "Anytime . . . but that doesn't mean I want to."

"What, are you scared now?"

"No way. I *said* I'd fight you. I only said I don't *want* to."

Spencer stepped back and lowered his fists. "You don't *want* to because you know I'd trash you."

"Not likely," Jared said. "You've been busting my chops all week. I'd be glad to smack you around. I just don't think it would solve anything. Like you said, we're supposed to be a team."

Spencer looked at Jared hard and nodded slowly. "Okay. For now. But this isn't over yet. You going to that game tonight?"

"I said I might."

"Maybe I'll see you there."

"Maybe you will. Tennis courts?"

"We'll see," Spencer said. "We'll see." He turned and walked away, and the other players joined him.

Jared watched them go until they'd left the school grounds. They were laughing. He looked around; no one else had been watching. He let out his breath and unclenched his fists. His ears were no longer cold.

Teammates, huh? he thought. *Some teammates. They give me no support in the game and nothing but grief afterward.*

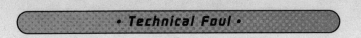

Jared wiped his nose with the back of his hand and walked across the blacktop toward home. It wasn't a long walk, but it was a lonely one. He decided to skip the high school game tonight. There was no sense in looking for trouble.

CHAPTER
5

Emotionally Drained

Coach Davis's rule was that if a player got kicked out of a game, then he had to sit out the next one as well. So Jared would have to wait an entire week before getting a chance for redemption.

He could practice with the team, of course, and things did seem a little better. The players were happy and relieved to have finally won a game, so no one—not even Spencer—was giving him a hard time. Coach did have Jared sit for part of the scrimmage, however, since the team would have to get ready to play without him in Thursday's game against Eastside.

So Jared sat in the bleachers and watched his teammates scrimmage. Coach had Tony Coccaro, a fifth grader, working with the first team. Tony was thin, but he was the tallest player on the team, so he might make up a bit for the loss of Jared's rebounding ability. There was a big difference between Tony and Jared as far as physical strength, however. If Eastside had a good inside game, then Hudson City would be in trouble.

Spencer's enthusiasm was obvious this afternoon, dishing out assists and shouting encouragement to his teammates, especially Tony. His passes were sharp and the first team dominated the scrimmage even without Jared, but tomorrow would probably be a different story.

After practice Jared took his time changing clothes and packing his gym bag. He wanted to wait until Spencer was gone before leaving the locker room. Yesterday had been draining for Jared—the technical foul, the ejection, the confrontation with Spencer—and he didn't want to face any more of that this afternoon. He hadn't known Coach's rule about sitting out a game until earlier today, and that had hit him hard as well. He certainly didn't feel like fighting.

Jared looked around the locker room. Only a few players were still there, but Spencer was one of them. Jared zipped up his gym bag and headed for the door. Spencer was looking the other way.

"Didn't see you last night," Spencer said softly as Jared walked past.

"Didn't feel like going," Jared said.

Spencer turned to look at him. "You didn't miss much," he said. "They lost."

"I heard."

"Tomorrow might not be pretty."

"How so?" Jared asked.

"My cousin goes to Eastside. She said they're big and tough. Our man Tony's gonna have his hands full under the basket. They'll eat him alive."

"Wish I could be in there," Jared said.

"Me, too."

Jared shook his head gently. "Stupid rule."

"Nah," Spencer said. "It's a good rule. Makes sense to me."

"Yeah, I guess," Jared said. "Might cost us a game though."

Spencer shrugged and reached into his locker for his backpack. "We'll be okay."

"My fault," Jared said.

"And mine."

They stood there for a few seconds; then Jared turned to go.

"Hold up," Spencer said. "I'll walk out with you."

Jared nodded, but he shifted his gym bag from his right hand to his left, just in case he'd need to throw a punch. Then Spencer followed him outside and onto the blacktop. A single lightbulb lit the area near the doorway. The rest of the school-yard was dark.

"Getting cold," Spencer said. Steam came out with his words.

"That's December," Jared replied, blowing out a stream of breath of his own.

"That's New Jersey," Spencer said. He looked up

at the sky, which had patchy gray clouds lit by moonlight. "Long winter ahead. We'd better start winning."

"Things'll be different as soon as I start playing again," Jared said. "Count on it."

"I will," Spencer said. He thrust his head toward home. "See you tomorrow, I guess. I gotta get going. My mom's making chicken. If I don't get there quick, my brothers will eat it all." He laughed. "And I'm starving!"

"Get moving then," Jared said with a smile. "I'll see you tomorrow. In school."

Jared watched Spencer hurry off. He could feel a difference already—a step in the right direction. Spencer wasn't a bad guy. They just needed to work together better. It was all a matter of thinking like a team. That would be easier if they started to like each other. That didn't seem impossible any longer.

Tonight's walk home was a lot less bleak than the night before's had been. Jared even took his time, heading up to the Boulevard to check out the Christmas lights downtown. Down the hill and across the river, he could see the New York City skyline, all lit up.

He felt lighter, more confident. They'd get this season turned around. They still had a long way to go.

Black, White, Purple, or Green

J ared opened the back door and greeted his
mom.

"How was practice?" she asked.

"Not bad," he said. "Pretty good. . . . Is Dad
home?"

"Not yet. He's bringing pizza, so we won't be
eating until he gets here. Have an apple or something."

"Sure."

Jared needed to tell his dad not to bother coming to the next day's game, since he wouldn't be
playing. With both of his parents working full

time, they didn't get to many of his sports events, so he didn't want his dad to waste any time off by watching Jared sit on the bench.

"You're working tomorrow, right?" he asked his mom.

"Yes. But I think your father's planning to get to the game," she said.

"Oh."

"We can't wait to see you play," she said. "I'll be sure to get to a game in the next week or so."

"That's good."

Jared hoped his dad hadn't scheduled the time off yet. And he didn't want to tell his mom about the suspension. He took a banana from the bowl on the counter and said, "See ya later." He went upstairs to his room.

Jared sat on his bed and turned on the radio, tuning in a classic rock station from New York City. He picked up his guitar from beside the bed and strummed a few chords along with one of the songs. He hadn't touched the guitar since last summer, when he'd quit taking lessons because of football practice. He'd promised his parents he'd start up again as soon as basketball ended. Mom and Dad often got on him about being "one dimensional." "It can't all be about sports," they said.

But for Jared, it mostly was.

Soon he heard his dad's car in the driveway.

"Pizza!" Mom yelled.

"I'm on my way!" Jared called back as he started down the stairs.

"Hey, Dad."

"Hey, Jag. Got your favorite food here."

"Smells great."

Dad took off his coat and hugged his wife. "Looks like I can slip out in time for the game tomorrow," he said. "Should be there by halftime, at least."

"Oh," Jared said. He peeled a slice of pizza out of the box and set it on his plate.

"You don't sound very enthused," Mom said.

"Well, it's like this . . . ," Jared began.

"Problem?" Dad asked.

"Well . . . I'm not playing tomorrow."

"What?" Mom said. "Did you get hurt?"

"No. Just . . . Coach said I have to sit out one

game. I kind of had an argument with somebody."

"Oh, boy," Dad said. He shook his head, but he was starting to smile. "An argument with your fists?"

"Not quite," Jared said. "Just a little pushing. But Coach has this rule . . ."

"Thank God he does," Mom said. "Did you get hurt?"

"No. I already said I didn't. It was nothing, Mom."

"Who was this fight with?" Mom asked.

"Spencer."

"That nice black kid?"

Jared rolled his eyes. "Yeah. That nice black kid. Mom, it was nothing. We're friends. You just get tense sometimes in the heat of a game. We're past it."

"Well, I'm glad the coach didn't let it slip by," she said. "A lot of coaches don't have that kind of integrity when their star players get in trouble."

"So, is Spencer suspended, too?" Dad asked.

"No. Just me, because I started it. But it's no big deal. Really."

"All right," Dad said. "Maybe I'll go to the game anyway. I'll check the schedule and see if I can get to another one next week. Maybe we can both go, huh, Sharon?"

"That would be nice," Mom said.

"Yeah," Jared said. "Believe me, we're gonna start winning again next week. I can feel it."

"All right," Mom said. "Case closed. Just one last question: This had nothing to do with Spencer's being black?"

"No way, Mom. Half the team is black. I would have pushed him if he was black, white, purple, or green. It was just a fight. And like I said, we're over it."

CHAPTER 7

A Lot to Prove

Jared felt sheepish sitting on the bench in street clothes, watching his teammates struggle against Eastside. As expected, Hudson City couldn't quite handle the opponent's inside strength, missing Jared's rebounding and shot-blocking skills. Although the Hornets kept the game close, Eastside gradually pulled away. When it was over, Hudson City's record had fallen to a dismal 1–4.

The players knew that they were better than their record, though, and the feeling in the locker room was that things were about to improve.

"If we'd had Jared out there, we would have won," Spencer said at the team meeting the next day. "I'm not complaining—I know why he wasn't there. What I'm saying is, all those other teams better watch out now. All that losing is behind us."

Spencer's prediction seemed true to anyone watching practice the rest of the week. The Hornets' team spirit soared. With Jared and Spencer leading the way, the scrimmages and drills took on a new level of energy and anticipation.

Finally, the next game arrived. Jared was so keyed up he could not concentrate at all in school. He looked at the clock repeatedly, counting down the minutes until he'd be out on the court again. He had a lot to prove. Not just about rebounding and putting the ball in the basket, but also about being a teammate.

Palisades was undefeated, with a pair of hot-shooting guards and a big, tough center. The Hudson City players were quiet on the bus ride over. Quiet but calm.

Jared sat next to Fiorelli. Spencer was in the

seat ahead of them, and as they approached the Palisades school, he knelt on the seat and turned to his teammates.

"I played against some of these guys last summer in a tournament," Spencer said. "Their center is strong as heck, but he's slow. You have to take advantage of that, Jared. We need to get the fast break going. Fiorelli and me can handle their guards; the deciding factor will be you."

Jared nodded. "Got ya," he said.

"We're in a hole as far as our record, but this will be a big step out of it," Spencer said. "No way we're gonna lose today, right?"

"No way," Jared answered.

"No way," repeated Fiorelli.

The bus came to a stop and the players filed off. The Palisades gym was already filling with students, and a small pep band was playing the Notre Dame fight song. Palisades players, in their black-and-gold warm-up suits, were running a layup drill at one of the baskets. The polished gym floor shined in the bright light. The scoreboard looked brand-new.

"We've only got about twenty minutes until game time," Coach Davis said. "Hit the locker room and get ready. I want you back out here in five."

Jared and the others set down their gym bags in the locker room and hustled back to the court. "Not giving us much time, are they?" Fiorelli commented.

"Who cares?" Jared said. "I'm ready right now. I haven't played a game in eight days. I'm practically leaping out of my skin."

Game time came quickly. The Palisades center out-jumped Jared for the opening tap, and their point guard nailed a quick three-pointer that brought the crowd to its feet. This wouldn't be easy.

Jared took the ball and tossed it in to Spencer.

"It's coming to you," Spencer said. "Let's see what you've got."

Spencer dribbled across midcourt and up to the top of the key. He passed off to Willie Shaw, but demanded the ball right back. Jared was near the basket, hounded by the Palisades center, who was at least two inches taller, and more muscular as well.

Spencer drove into the lane, then flicked a bounce pass in to Jared. Jared pumped, making a move toward the basket. His opponent lunged hard to that side, and Jared deftly pivoted as the defender lost his balance. With a wide-open path now, Jared took one dribble and leaped toward the basket, laying the ball off the backboard and into the hoop.

The Hornets hustled back on defense. Fiorelli and Spencer stuck close to the guards, having already seen the evidence of their long-range shooting skills. The point guard fired up another three-pointer anyway, but it struck the rim and bounded away. Jared grabbed it and fired an outlet pass to Spencer.

"Gotta move!" Spencer yelled to Jared as he took off, dribbling at full speed. Jared ran straight up the court as well, easily leaving his defender behind. As Jared reached the free-throw line, Spencer hit him with a dead-on bounce pass that Jared gathered in without breaking stride. He took one easy dribble and found the hoop for another layup. Hudson City had the lead.

"Beautiful," Spencer said as they ran back. "All day, Jared. We can make that play all day."

A groan came from the crowd and Jared turned back toward the basket. Fiorelli was trotting up the court with his fist in the air, shouting, "Yeah!" The scoreboard turned from 4–3 to 6–3. Fiorelli must have stolen the ball and scored.

Palisades quickly signaled for a time-out. Spencer patted Jared on the back and they ran to the sideline.

"What did you do?" Jared asked Fiorelli.

"Snuck in there on the in-bounds pass," Fiorelli said with a bigger grin than usual. "The guy wasn't even looking. Easy steal."

"Way to go."

Palisades took better care of the ball after that, and the score stayed close throughout the first half. Jared scored twice more on fast breaks, but the other Palisades players made up for their center's slowness and hurried back after missed shots. Their guards also kept shooting from outside, and many of those shots hit the target. By halftime, Hudson City led, 25–23, and Jared had scored ten points.

"We're wearing them down," Coach Davis said in the locker room. "We need to keep running, right, Spence?"

Spencer nodded. "Look for the fast break off every defensive rebound we get," he said. "Jared—keep hustling. We're getting five-on-four or five-on-three breaks every time we run; that center can't get down the court fast enough. Sooner or later they're all gonna fold."

"That's right," said Coach. "They're already tired. We've got to take advantage of that."

The halftime break let Palisades get some rest, and they kept the game close early in the third quarter. But then Fiorelli hit a wide-open three-pointer from the corner, and the Palisades point guard tried to answer in a hurry.

The shot looked good, but it struck the back of the rim and bounded high into the air. Jared grabbed it as it came down, found Spencer for the outlet pass, and sprinted up the court. Just as before, Spencer made a soft little bounce pass to the wide-open Jared, and Jared laid it off the backboard and in.

"Press!" shouted Spencer, seeing a chance to capitalize. The Hudson City players converged on their opponents, guarding them tightly as Jared hounded the man with the ball, who was desperately trying to find someone to pass to. He tried to throw it high and long, but Jared deflected the ball and it popped into the air in front of the basket. Willie Shaw raced in and caught it on the run, taking one dribble and scoring.

Suddenly Hudson City led by nine. Palisades called time-out. The Hornets trotted triumphantly to their bench.

"They're dead meat now," Spencer said in the huddle. "We're gonna run 'em right out of their own fancy gym."

"No letting up," Jared said fiercely. "No way they get back in this game. This is *our* season. This is where it starts. Let's finish these guys off and move on to the next one."

Palisades brought in a substitute for their center. He was shorter but much quicker. It made little difference; Jared dominated the boards and Hudson City continued to run. By the time Jared came out of the game with less than two minutes to play, he'd scored a game-high 27 points. Hudson City was ahead by fourteen.

Jared was about to step out of the locker room into the narrow hallway that led to the exit. He hesitated when he heard his name, and eavesdropped on Ryan and Fiorelli, who were talking out in the hall.

"Coach must have said something to Spence and Jared," Ryan was saying. "Ever since that fight on the court, they've been like best buddies."

"It wasn't Coach. They settled it themselves," Fiorelli said. "I was there. They're outside after the Emerson game and Spence was like, 'You smack me on the court and you think I'm gonna just let that slide?' And Jared's like, 'It was justified, dude.' And Spence says, 'Yeah, well we can settle this thing at the tennis courts tonight, man, and then we'll see.' And Jared is going, 'Anytime, pal, anytime.' And then they just stared each other down. You could see the steam coming out of their ears. But then they just backed away, real slow, and since then there's been a kind of truce. I don't know if it'll last though. It better."

"Whatever happened, it worked," Ryan said. "We're looking good right now."

Jared pushed open the door and grinned at his teammates. "What are you guys jamming about?" he asked.

"Nothing," Fiorelli said. "Just saying that if we can keep you and Spencer from clobbering each other, we should be okay."

"More than okay," Jared said. "We're over the hump now. We'll cruise from here."

"Don't get overconfident," Fiorelli said. "Just keep it up. One game at a time, man."

"You said it."

Team Chemistry

J ared was shooting baskets in the driveway on Saturday afternoon, dodging a few frozen puddles. He'd definitely found his touch, scoring 24 points the day before in a big win over South Bergen. That was the team that had pounded Hudson City in the season opener, and this victory was a sure sign that things had turned around. They had five more regular-season games, three of them against teams they'd lost to earlier. At 3–4, they couldn't afford many more losses if they hoped to make the playoffs.

Jared dribbled in place away from the basket,

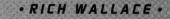

up near the back door of the house. He took a quick step and a dribble left, then drove hard to his right and went in for a layup.

"Check out that move!" came a yell from the sidewalk.

Jared looked up to find Fiorelli and Spencer walking his way, grinning. "Let's see that ball," said Spencer, holding out his hands.

Jared sent an overhand pass in Spencer's direction. Spence grabbed it, made a quick dribble between his legs, and sent a long shot toward the basket. The ball rolled around the rim and fell out.

"What are you guys doing on this side of town?" Jared asked.

"Just slumming," Fiorelli said. "See how the other half lives."

"Oh yeah," Jared said, rolling his eyes. "Over here on Society Hill."

"We just thought we'd see what you were up to," Spencer said, tossing the ball back to Jared. "Make sure you weren't getting into trouble."

"Just working out," Jared said.

"You never stop, huh?"

"Not much. It pays off."

"I hear you," Spencer said.

Jared didn't get many visitors. He wasn't a total loner, but he never minded keeping his own company. Spencer and Fiorelli lived across town and had never been to Jared's house.

"So, you up for hanging out a bit?" Fiorelli said.

"Sure. Where to?"

"I don't know," Fiorelli said. "You got any money?"

"Some."

"Could hit one of the pizza places on the Boulevard or something," Spencer said. "They got video games at Villa Roma."

"Sounds good to me. Come on in for a minute."

They entered the house. Jared's mom was at the computer in the family room.

"Company," Jared called.

"Who's that?" Mom answered.

"Guys from the team," Jared said. "We're going to Villa Roma. Okay?"

"Of course," she said, entering the kitchen. She smiled when she saw Fiorelli and Spencer. "Hi

Jason. Spencer," she said. "I hear you guys are playing some great basketball."

"Yeah, finally," Spencer said. "We finally got the chemistry going."

"Yeah," Mom said. She smiled and flicked up her eyebrows. "I heard there were some problems."

Spencer looked down and gave an embarrassed grin. "We worked it out." He looked up and rolled his eyes. "Peacefully."

"I'm glad," she said. She grabbed her purse from the counter and took out some bills. "Let me treat. Pizza and wings, huh? I guess I don't have to worry about making supper."

"Thanks, Mom," Jared said. "I'll be back whenever."

"Take your time. Have fun, Jared. . . . With your friends."

Villa Roma was the most kid-friendly pizza place in town, with two large TV screens—one showing music videos and the other always tuned to a sports network. One wall was lined with pinball and video games, and soda refills were free.

Two players from the high school varsity team were sitting at a table near the entrance as Jared, Spencer, and Fiorelli walked in. One of them gave a nod of recognition to the younger guys.

"Hello, men," Fiorelli said. "Fellow hoopsters."

The older players laughed. The one that had frizzy red hair and was wearing a letterman's jacket gave them a thumbs-up. The other guy was staring at the television above the counter, which was showing a college basketball game.

Spencer led the way to the counter and ordered a large pizza and a dozen wings. "And a pitcher of Coke," Jared added. "Three glasses."

They moved toward an old Space Invaders game near the back of the restaurant and piled their coats on the floor. Spencer put some quarters in the game. He glanced up toward the front and whispered, "I don't think I'd be wearing my letterman's jacket if I was on *that* team. I wouldn't be advertising."

Fiorelli laughed. "Their record is even worse than ours. What are they, two and nine or some-

thing?"

"Something like that," Spencer said. "I don't think they've had a winning season in ten years. This just ain't enough of a basketball town. Not yet."

Fiorelli nodded. "We'll change that. Once our man Jared puts some meat on his bones and you grow a few inches taller." Fiorelli made a shooting motion, tossing an imaginary basketball toward an imaginary hoop. "We'll be the ones who change things. Just like we've turned this season around."

"Not quite yet," Jared cautioned. "Like you said, buddy. One game at a time."

"Yeah," Spencer said. "We still have a tough road ahead. Palisades won't let us run like that next time, I guarantee. They'll come up with some way to slow us down. Next time will be a shoot-out, not a track meet."

"And they've got the big guns," Fiorelli added.

"We've just got to keep our heads together," Spencer said. "Think about every situation. We might not be big, but we're smart. We can figure out how to win."

The guy at the counter called over that their food was ready, so they went to collect it. They took a table a ways from the high school players, who had been joined by two other teenagers.

"You know what game is next, don't you, Jared?" Spencer asked.

"Yeah. I know."

"Memorial," Fiorelli said flatly.

"I said I know." Jared stopped chewing for a second. Memorial was the game he'd lost almost single-handedly, with his awful fourth-quarter shooting and that missed shot at the final buzzer. He didn't need reminding.

"Monday," Spencer said. "You been thinking about it?"

"Yeah," Jared said. "Thinking. Not worrying. That was a long time ago."

"Couple of weeks," Fiorelli said.

"So what? We just beat the two best teams in the league. That's way in the past."

"I thought *we* were the best team," Spencer

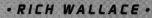

said.

"You know what I mean," Jared answered. "They're in first and second. Memorial's up there, too. I'm ready."

"Just making sure," Spencer said. "We can't afford any regression."

"Come on, guys. I've been playing great. Is this why you dragged me here? To bust my chops and put pressure on me?"

"No," Spencer said. "No way. It just came up. Forget it."

"Yeah, forget it," Fiorelli said. "You're right. We gotta look forward, not behind us."

Jared set down his pizza and nodded. Forward was the only way to go.

Get Me the Ball

The rematch with Memorial was crucial for Hudson City. Memorial was ahead of them in the standings, and almost certainly headed for the league playoffs. The Hornets had to get a win.

Jared and his teammates were unusually quiet while warming up, concentrating on the game ahead. Jared was nervous. He didn't want a repeat of the previous game, when he'd turned to ice in the fourth quarter and cost his team the game.

Memorial's gym was small, and the wooden bleachers—packed with students—came right up to the edge of the court. This wouldn't be an easy place to play. Already the Memorial fans were playfully taunting the Hudson City players.

"Block it out," Spencer said in the team huddle before the opening tap. "They can make all the noise they want—the game takes place on the court."

Jared took a deep breath and let it out. He looked at the opposing center, waiting in the mid-court circle for the jump ball. The kid was taller than Jared but not bulky. His arms were long and thin. Jared had been dominant against him for most of that first game, but the man had shut Jared down when he'd needed to score toward the end.

Jared took his place and leaped as the referee tossed up the ball. The Memorial center got there first, tapping the ball back to a guard, who took control and began to dribble.

"Defense!" shouted Spencer. Jared made his way into the key near the basket, finding the Memorial center and getting between him and the hoop. The guy hadn't scored much last time— Memorial had won it with outside shooting—but

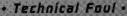

somehow he seemed more confident this time, more ready to take charge. He was shouting for the ball, his arms raised high above his head.

The pass came in, and Jared planted his feet, refusing to yield any ground. The Memorial center pivoted and took one dribble, then jumped high and lofted the ball over Jared's outstretched arms. The ball fell cleanly through the net, and Memorial had taken the early lead.

He didn't make a single shot like that last time, Jared thought. *He's been working, that's for sure.*

Ryan Grimes missed a short jumper for Hudson City, and Memorial grabbed the ball and ran. Spencer and Fiorelli hustled back, halting the fast break, but Memorial pulled back and set up its offense, with the point guard calling for a play.

It was a simple play. The center cut across the key and around a teammate as Jared followed. But Jared couldn't get through the screen set up by the other Memorial player, and the center wound up wide open for an eight-foot jump shot from the baseline. Again the ball fell softly into the basket, and the Memorial crowd went nuts.

"What got into him?" Spencer said as he dribbled upcourt alongside Jared. "He didn't do that last time."

"No kidding," Jared said. "It won't last. I won't let it."

But things did not get easier. The Memorial center continued his hot shooting throughout the first half, scoring fourteen points before intermission to lead his team to a 31–24 advantage. Jared had scored ten, but he'd also picked up two fouls. He'd have to be careful not to foul out.

"We're still in this game, boys," Coach Davis said at halftime. "We need to make a run in the third quarter and put some pressure on them. Jared, their center is bound to cool off sooner or later. Stay in his face. No easy shots."

"I think his arms must have grown six inches since last time," Jared said. "He's been getting way up over me on those jumpers."

Coach laughed. "I think he just learned how to use his size," he said. "They're a better team than they were. Good coaching, I guess."

Spencer got hot in the third quarter, connecting

on a pair of three-pointers and two fast-break layups. Hudson City cut the lead to four points, then one. By the time the fourth quarter started, it was all even.

"It's attitude now," Spencer said at the bench. "Who wants it more? Let's put these guys away. Let's go."

The teams battled back and forth, exchanging the lead. Jared scored on two consecutive possessions, making tough layups with his defender all over his back.

"The guy's holding my shirt!" Jared called to the referee as he raced downcourt after scoring. "Can't you see that?"

The referee did not respond. But Willie Shaw did. Willie was the quietest guy on the team, but he spoke up to Jared. "Watch your mouth," he said. "Keep your head on."

Jared decided to dish it right back. The Memorial center got the ball in the key and drove to shoot. Jared leaned hard into him and pushed at his elbow. The shot went in anyway. And then came the whistle.

"Number thirty-three, red," said the official. Foul on Jared. The spectators stood and yelled, jeering at Jared and pointing with a chant of "You! You! You!"

Jared stared at the high ceiling for a second, then brought his head down and mouthed a curse word. Spencer grabbed his arm and said, "No biggie. Just keep at it."

That was Jared's third foul. About three minutes remained. The free throw was good, and Memorial led, 48–46.

They'll pay for that, Jared thought. *Just get me the ball. I'll clobber 'em.*

Memorial tightened its defense, and Spencer and Fiorelli worked the ball around outside. Jared and the Memorial center kept battling under the basket, with Jared working to get open and his opponent hounding him.

"Let go of me," Jared said, swatting at the defender's hand, which had a grip on Jared's jersey. "Quit cheating."

Spencer unleashed a long three-point attempt,

but the ball smacked off the rim. Jared leaped high for the rebound. He got his hands on it, but the Memorial center batted it away. Fiorelli dove for the loose ball and called time-out before falling out of bounds.

The team huddled up. "What's going on in there, Jared?" Coach Davis asked.

"The guy's all over me," Jared said sharply. "He's holding my shirt, he's elbowing me. Every time I get the ball, he's fouling me. And they're not calling anything."

The Memorial spectators were mostly standing and stomping their feet. Coach Davis looked at the bleachers and shook his head. "In a hostile environment, you have to keep your cool," he said. "Keep working now. Be smart."

They broke the huddle and walked onto the court. "Great advice," Spencer said to Jared with a little smile. "'Be smart.' Like we don't know that?"

"Coach does what he can," Jared said. "He doesn't know much basketball, but he knows how to stay calm."

When the ball came to Jared he backed hard into his defender as both players pushed. Jared dribbled and feinted left, then jumped high and banked the ball off the backboard. It fell safely into the basket, tying the score.

The Memorial point guard answered with a driving layup. Jared inbounded the ball to Spencer. Memorial was pressing now, picking up their opponents in the backcourt and sticking close. Spencer dribbled quickly around Fiorelli's screen, then tossed the ball to Grimes at midcourt. Things were getting tight now. Less than two minutes remained.

Jared raced up and took his position near the basket. Again he felt the hand on his back, again he swatted it away. Spencer's pass came in. Jared was under the basket and his opponent was all over him. There was no shot, but Jared spotted Fiorelli in the corner and fired it out to him. Jared stepped into key, calling for the ball back. He felt a sharp blow to his shoulder, and turned and jabbed his elbow hard into his opponent's chest.

And there came the whistle, sharp and long. "That's a *T*!" the referee shouted, pointing at Jared. "Thirty-three, red, with the elbow."

Jared felt a chill and all the air seemed to go out of him. He'd lost his temper at a critical point, and now Memorial, leading by two, would shoot a free throw and then get the ball.

"Not again," Jared said to himself. He couldn't cost his team another game.

The horn sounded, and Tony Coccaro came onto the court, pointing at Jared. He was out of the game. Jared walked slowly to the bench as the spectators hooted him loudly.

"Sit here," Coach said, pointing to the spot next to him. Jared sat down and stared at the floor.

"Just take a breather," Coach said. "This isn't over. You're going back in as soon as we get the ball."

Jared nodded. Memorial made the technical free throw and set up to inbound the ball near midcourt. The scoreboard clock read 1:17. Plenty of time. Memorial led, 51–48.

Spencer shadowed the point guard, not letting

him penetrate. Jared kept his eyes on Coccaro, who was overmatched by the Memorial center but was managing to guard him closely. Fiorelli was playing off from his man a step, keeping half an eye on the situation near the basket, ready to help out if the ball went inside.

Spencer forced his man to stop dribbling, and he sent a long pass toward the center. Fiorelli raced over and nabbed it, intercepting the pass and keeping Hudson City alive.

Fiorelli passed to Spencer, who dribbled upcourt quickly. He stopped as he crossed the midcourt line and glanced at Coach Davis, who was signaling for him to call time-out. Spencer did.

"Great defense," Coach said. "Tony, you did what we needed. You're out."

Jared was already at the scorer's table, reporting back in. As he stepped onto the court, the spectators let him have it again.

"Mr. T!" came the cry. "Sharpen up those elbows!"

Jared winced, but they wouldn't get to him this time. Fiorelli put his arm across Jared's shoulder.

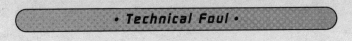

"Let's shut them up, Jared. Let's do it!"

Spencer and Fiorelli passed the ball back and forth, taking their time. Then Spencer drove into the lane, spurting past his defender, toward the basket. The Memorial center stepped away from Jared, blocking Spencer's path. Spencer gave a quick little juke and fired a bounce pass to Jared, who was wide open under the basket. Jared laid it up and in.

Hudson City had cut the lead to one point. This defensive sequence would make the difference. "Stop 'em!" came Spencer's cry.

Half a minute remained. The ball came in to the Memorial center. He turned and faked to his left, but Jared had been watching that move all day. When the center pivoted to his right to shoot, Jared was ready. He leaped and blocked the shot, swatting it cleanly toward the sideline. Spencer got to it first, and Hudson City had a chance to win.

Spencer dribbled past midcourt and called Hudson City's final time-out.

"Get the ball inside," Coach Davis said in the

huddle. He tapped Jared's chest with a finger. "We're putting this on you, Jared. You win this game for us. You do it."

Jared swallowed hard, but he wasn't nervous. He wanted that ball. *Let the guy grab me,* Jared thought. *Let him foul me, let him try to stop me. I'm going to score.*

"De-*fense!*" came the chant from the bleachers. "De-*fense!*"

And when the ball came to Jared, he did what he needed to do. Up and over his defender, who pushed back and grunted, leaving his feet and reaching toward the backboard. Jared's shot was clean and sure, drifting above his opponent's hands and into the basket. Hudson City was back in the lead.

Memorial frantically brought the ball up with the seconds ticking away. A long shot at the buzzer fell short. The spectators were suddenly silent.

Jared pumped his fist and hugged Spencer. Hudson City was back in business.

"That's it. That's the Hudson City way," said

Fiorelli as they walked off the court. "They're like, 'We'll stuff these guys. We can hold and foul and talk trash all day,' and we're like, 'Talk all you want. We'll put it right back in your face.'"

Fiorelli turned to Jared and gave him a hard high five. "That's right, *Mr. T*!" he said. "You! You! You! You showed 'em. You did."

Jared didn't say anything. He just smiled broadly and shook his coach's hand as the team made its way to the bus.

CHAPTER
10

Taking
a Break

Hudson City followed that win with two
more, improving their record to 6–4 and
moving into playoff contention. With five straight
victories, every team in the conference had taken
notice of the Hornets. Two games remained—the
rematch with Palisades and the regular season
finale against Emerson. They'd beaten both teams
earlier, but there were no easy wins in this league.
The top four teams would make the playoffs. The
standings stood like this.

	W	L
South Bergen	7	3
Palisades	7	3
Memorial	6	4
Hudson City	6	4
Eastside	5	5
Lincoln	2	8
Emerson	2	8

Jared's parents were waiting outside for him after the win over Eastside.

"That was worth waiting for," Mom said as Jared got into the backseat of the car. "I wish we could get to more of the games. If you make the playoffs, we'll certainly get to those."

"Well, as long as we split our next two, we should get in," Jared said.

"You played a great game," Dad said. "And you lost to those guys last time?"

"I didn't play last time, remember?" Jared said. "That was my suspension."

"Oh, yeah," Dad said. "Well, you made up for it today."

Jared had scored 18 points and grabbed 11 rebounds as Hudson City rolled to the win. He was still averaging over 20 points a game, even though he was shooting a bit less. He was taking better shots and getting more assists by passing to his teammates.

"Let's eat out," Dad said. "Hamburgers okay with everybody?"

"Sure," said Jared. "Sounds good."

What a difference a couple of weeks had made. The Hudson City team had gone from being a frustrated group of players to league-championship contenders. And Jared had gone from outcast to leader, with two new friends in Spencer and Fiorelli. Things were definitely looking up.

There was a tough road ahead though. The rematch with Palisades was next. And even though it was a home game for Hudson City, Jared knew Palisades would be gunning for revenge. Then, if they made the playoffs, things would get even hotter.

"This is one tough league," Jared said. "No such thing as an easy game."

"You wouldn't want it any other way, would you?" Dad asked. "You always want to be testing yourself. That's how you get better."

"Yeah," Jared said. "I know."

Dad turned the car into the restaurant parking lot. For once, Jared was getting a little tired of talking about basketball. "How's work going, Mom?" he asked.

Mom turned back with a surprised smile. "You've never asked me about work in your life," she said. "It's fine." She raised her eyebrows. "What makes you ask?"

"Just changing the subject," Jared said. "Sometimes a guy thinks about things other than sports, you know?"

"Sometimes," Mom answered. "That just hasn't been the case with you."

Jared nodded and grinned. "This has been a tough season. About time I took a break, at least for one evening."

At home, Jared climbed the stairs to his room and took out his guitar. He'd started playing late last winter, and by spring the instructor had asked him to take part in a recital at the community center. Jared had only advanced enough to pluck out a simple version of Beethoven's "Ode to Joy" at the recital, but by summer he was playing acceptable versions of some rock songs.

Jared began strumming. He was rusty, but it came back quickly. Despite a few mistakes, he hadn't lost much skill since summer.

After a while there was a knock on his door, and Dad stuck his head in. "Haven't heard that in a long time," he said.

Jared stopped strumming. "Just jamming a little," he said. "It's relaxing."

"You ready to get back into it, Jag?"

Jared shrugged. "Soon. After basketball season. I can only concentrate on one big thing at a time."

"That's understandable," Dad said. "If you're going to do something, do it right."

"That's what I figure," Jared said. He strummed a couple of chords. "One thing at a time. One direction."

Out of
Their Game

*T*he Hudson City gym was packed this time. A win would move the Hornets into a tie for second place, but a loss could jeopardize their chances to make the playoffs.

Palisades was clearly psyched up for the game, with the players smacking each other's backs and shouting enthusiastically as they shot layups down at their basket. They wanted to avenge that first loss to Hudson City. A lot of Palisades fans had made the trip. They'd even brought along their pep band, which was blaring the theme from *Rocky*.

"Thought this was a *home* game," Spencer said to Jared as they stretched on the side of the court. "I think they've got more people here than we do."

"Just block it out, like we always do," Jared said. "We've got fans here." He looked up at the bleachers. "Some."

"I'm kidding," Spencer said. "Besides, we kicked their butts in their own gym last time. No way they beat us in ours."

"No way," Jared said. But he did feel uneasy when he glanced back at the Palisades players. They were energized. They were definitely not intimidated one bit by being the visiting team, or by the fact that they'd lost to Hudson City already. They looked like a team on a mission.

"Huddle up!" called Coach Davis, and the players trotted to the bench. Coach was much more in command these days. The winning streak had boosted his confidence as much as the players'. And he had learned a lot, being smart enough to listen to team leaders like Spencer and Fiorelli, but wise enough to know when they were wrong.

"Remember to run on these guys," Coach said.

"Our fast break ran them ragged last time, fellas. Let's do it again."

But it was clear from the start that Palisades was determined not to let that happen. With the score tied early on, Jared grabbed a defensive rebound and quickly hit Spencer with an outlet pass. Jared then ran hard downcourt, eluding the Palisades center, who did not have the speed to stay with him.

"Right here!" Jared said as he crossed midcourt and headed into the key. Spencer's bounce pass was right on target, but Jared never got to it. Leon Johnson, the Palisades' point guard, stepped in front and stole the ball. He took two quick dribbles and threw a long pass to their center, who was wide open in the backcourt. He easily dribbled in and scored.

The second fast-break opportunity came a few minutes later, when the Palisades center missed a shot and Jared hauled in the rebound. Again he found Spencer with the pass, and again he raced toward the opposite basket.

But this time the pass didn't come. Spencer

pulled back when he saw that Jared was tightly covered by Johnson. Instead, he dribbled out beyond the three-point line and eventually passed to Fiorelli.

By then, Palisades had all five players back on defense.

At the break between the first and second quarters, Coach Davis pointed out what had happened. "They're matching up differently when we try to run," he said. "They're trying to buy time until their center gets down there to play defense, so they've got their quickest player shadowing Jared. But somebody has to be open, right? Who's being left alone?"

Ryan Grimes said, "Usually me." Ryan wasn't much of a scorer, but he was one of the team's best defensive players.

"See, they learned something from that last game," Coach said. "They're making sure not to leave our scorers open on the break. So look for the open man. Ryan, if no one's on you, get into the key. You may get a couple of easy baskets. Then they'll have to adjust. If we keep running on 'em, there'll usually be at least one man open."

Palisades went on a hot-shooting tear in the second quarter, so Hudson City had few opportunities to utilize the fast break. By halftime Palisades had built a 27–20 lead.

"We've got to try something different," Spencer said. "They're nailing three-pointers. So can we. A couple of treys and we're back in it."

"That's not our game," Jared said. "We run. We hammer the ball inside. Stick to that and we'll break these guys down, just like last time."

"We'll see," Spencer said.

Spencer did come out gunning in the second half, but the strategy didn't work. Spencer hit only one three-pointer in the third quarter and missed four of them. The Palisades' lead grew to double digits.

Jared grabbed Spencer's arm during a time-out. "We're totally out of our game," he said. "We're a team, remember? No heroes?"

Spencer nodded. "I was just trying to get us back into it," he said.

The fourth quarter went better, but the lead was

too much to overcome. Spencer started feeding the ball inside, and Jared scored readily from close range. Hudson City cut into the lead, whittling it down to four points in the final minute. But a clutch three-point shot by Leon Johnson sealed the game for Palisades.

"Man, we should have won," Fiorelli said in the somber locker room after.

"We have to stick to our game," Jared said. "They stopped us from running, but that isn't all we're about. If the fast break doesn't work, we have to get the ball inside. We lost our heads in the second half and dug a hole. When we finally got back to our game, we at least made it close."

"We just ran out of time," Coach Davis said. "I think we learned that we can beat that team in more ways than one. And we may see them again in the playoffs."

Jared walked across the room and took a seat on the bench next to Spencer. "You okay?" he said to Spencer, who was staring glumly into his locker.

Spencer shrugged. "I blew that one, man. I panicked. When they built that lead, I kept trying to make some big statement. Score some points in a hurry. If I'd just been patient, we would have been all right."

"Listen, you've been a big reason why we went on that winning streak," Jared said. "As long as we learned something today, then we'll be fine. I've got a feeling we'll see these guys again."

Spencer nodded and tossed one of his sneakers into the locker. "I hate losing," he said. "Especially when I know we should have won."

A Night Out

H udson City defeated Emerson in the final regular season game, clinching a spot in the playoffs. The Hornets would meet South Bergen in the first game of a Saturday-afternoon playoff doubleheader at Palisades, with the home ·team taking on Memorial in the second game. The winners would meet Monday night at Palisades to decide the title.

Ironically, each of the four teams in the playoffs had one loss and one win against each of the others. There was no telling who would emerge as the champion.

Friday's practice was easy, with the Hornets running some basic passing and shooting drills and then scrimmaging lightly for about half an hour. As they left the court, Spencer fell in step with Jared.

"Got a few people coming over tonight," Spencer said. "Just to hang out, maybe shoot some pool in the basement. You up for it?"

"Definitely," Jared said.

"I figure we should stick together tonight," Spencer said. "Minimize the distractions, you know? Keep the focus right where it should be. On the team."

"Yeah. Should I bring anything?"

"I don't know. You could pick up some pretzels or chips if you want. My mom's making sandwiches and cake. We'll have plenty of food."

"Sounds great, Spence. I'll be there."

The night was cold, but Jared felt warm as he walked along the Boulevard toward Spencer's house. Most of the stores were closed at this hour, but the small restaurants and pizza places were open. Jared wasn't much of a night guy; he spent most evenings at home with his parents. Getting invited to Spencer's had been a nice surprise.

Jared reached St. Joseph's Church at Ninth Street and crossed over to the small grocery store on the corner. He walked down the fruit-and-vegetable aisle toward the back of the store. There was a big variety of chips and other snacks on the shelves back there. Jared picked up a large bag of barbecue potato chips and shook it gently to make sure it was full. Then he felt a poke in the back.

"What are you doing here?" Jared asked when he turned and saw Fiorelli's signature grin.

"Getting some soda," Fiorelli said. "You headed to Spence's place?"

"Yeah. You?"

"Yeah. Didn't want to show up empty-handed."

"Me, either," Jared said.

They paid for the snacks and headed out together. Spencer's house was just a couple of blocks away.

"Big one tomorrow," Fiorelli said as they walked along.

"No kidding," Jared said. "Everybody says the playoffs are different. More intense and pressurized."

"Seems to be true," Fiorelli said. "Hard to tell in this town. Hasn't been much playoff excitement around here for a long time."

Spencer's mother answered the door. "Hello Jason," she said, smiling at Fiorelli. "Hello," she said to Jared.

"Hi, Mrs. Lewis. I'm Jared."

Jared stuck out his hand and she took it in both of hers. "Oh, yes," she said. "Spencer's mentioned you a lot. Come on in, boys. The others are downstairs."

The other three starters and a couple of subs were there. All were sixth graders. The cellar was small and crowded, but somehow they'd managed to fit in a pool table. A game was under way, and music was playing from a portable CD player.

"Welcome, gentlemen," Spencer said as Jared and Fiorelli came down the stairs. "One rule: no basketball talk tonight. We need to relax. We'll have all morning to get psyched for the game.

Tonight we avoid the pressure."

"Good deal," Jared said.

"Fine by me," added Fiorelli.

"All right," Spencer said, chalking up his cue. "You two are up next against me and Willie. As soon as we finish this one off."

"Black against white?" Fiorelli said, faking surprise.

"Hey, that's the way of the world," Spencer said, smiling. "It's all equal on the billiards table. Basketball court, too."

Fiorelli grinned and nodded. "I hear you. No basketball talk, though, remember?"

"Okay," Spencer said. "New subject. Somebody told me Amanda asked you out yesterday."

Fiorelli blushed and rolled his eyes. "It's like this, Spence," he said. Then he hesitated. It was no secret that a lot of girls had crushes on Fiorelli, with his all-American-boy good looks and sense of humor. As of yet, he hadn't made any kind of move, however.

"Like *what*?" Spencer asked slyly.

"She comes up to me after the Emerson game,

and she's like all friendly and everything, like 'Oh, you played great.' And I'm like, 'Thanks, I know,' even though I had, like, my worst game in a month. And she's going, 'We should go celebrate. I'll buy you some pizza.' And I'm like, 'My mom's making spaghetti. I'm already late.' So she acts all disappointed, and she's rubbing my arm and going, 'How about tomorrow night?'"

"Tonight?" Spencer said. "So what are you doing *here*, my man? She's cute."

"Oh, *man*," Fiorelli said. "I told her I had plans. You know, to come over here. So she goes, 'Is Spencer having a party?' And I go, 'Yeah.' But then I go, 'No. No. It ain't a party really. Just guys from the team.' And she's like, 'What fun will that be? Just guys?'"

"So what are you saying?" Spencer asked. "She's coming here?"

"I don't know. Maybe. But she wouldn't come alone. She'd bring other girls."

"Well, if they show up, they'll have to squeeze in here with the rest of us," Spencer said. "The maximum capacity of this cellar is about six people, and we're over the limit now."

Jared was hoping the girls wouldn't show up. He'd been looking forward to a fun evening with the team. Girls would only complicate matters. And, unlike Fiorelli and Spencer, he had no idea how to talk to girls anyway.

Spencer and Willie won the first game of eight ball, then Jared and Fiorelli beat Ryan Grimes and Louie Gonzalez. Spencer's mom opened the cellar door and called down, "Spencer. More visitors."

Spencer looked at Fiorelli, who frowned and shrugged. "Be right up," Spencer said. He and Fiorelli went upstairs.

"Man," said Willie after they'd gone. "I hope they don't bring those girls down here. Certain times, you just want to be with your boys. This night was supposed to be about getting rid of distractions. If girls aren't distractions, I don't know what is."

They played three more games of pool before Spencer and Fiorelli came back down, alone.

"Got rid of 'em," Spencer said. "No problem."

"Yeah *right*," Fiorelli said, shaking his head.

"No problem for you."

"Aw," Spencer said, bursting into a giant smile. "Listen, Jason, you made the big sacrifice for the team. And we all appreciate it, don't we guys?"

"What do we appreciate?" Jared asked.

"Jason here agreed to take Amanda to the movies tomorrow night after we beat South Bergen," Spencer said. "It was the only way to get them to leave."

"You're the man, Fiorelli," said Willie.

"Yeah, I'm the man," Fiorelli said. "How do I get into these things anyway?"

"You're just too good-looking," Spencer said. "You need to get your face messed up or something. Maybe take an elbow in the jaw during the game."

Fiorelli blushed again. "Let's get down to business," he said, picking up a pool cue. "Me and Jared. We'll take on anybody."

Yeah, thought Jared. *Pool or basketball, I'll take on the world. That's enough, for now.*

Playoff Pressure

"**G**otta admit, this is a great atmosphere for basketball," Spencer said as the Hudson City players took to the floor at the Palisades gym. Spectators from all four of the playoff teams had filled the bleachers, and music was blaring from the speakers.

South Bergen was already warming up at one of the baskets, and the players from Palisades and Memorial were sitting on opposite sides of the court, high up in the bleachers, waiting their turn.

"Big advantage for Palisades, getting to have the playoffs at home," Jared said.

"All the other gyms in the league are too small," Spencer said. "It's no problem. We know we can win on the road."

Jared nodded and looked around the gym.

"Don't get psyched out," Spencer said. "This is what we've been playing for. Pressure's good."

"Pressure's our friend," said Fiorelli. He poked Jared in the chest. "'You! You! You!' Remember? We thrive in hostile environments."

"Yeah," said Jared. "We do."

South Bergen came out shooting, nailing a couple of three-pointers in the early going. Hudson City kept things close with a powerful inside game. Spencer was effective working the ball in to Jared, and Jared hit his first three shots.

"All day," Spencer said to Jared as they walked toward the bench during a time-out. "That ball keeps coming to you in there."

"Don't be surprised if they start doubling up on Jared," Coach Davis said. "Look for the open man. Keep getting it inside while we're able to, but sooner or later they're going to make an adjustment."

Just as Coach said, Jared found himself double-teamed on Hudson City's next possession. Spencer got the ball in to him, but a forward darted over to help, leaving Fiorelli alone in the corner. Jared pumped to shoot, then fired the ball out to Jason, who hit the wide-open three-pointer.

"We've got too many weapons," Spencer said as they sprinted back on defense. "They leave Jason open, he'll slaughter them. They leave just one man on Jared, he'll eat 'em up inside."

South Bergen kept making adjustments, having other players help out on Jared, bringing in fresh players to try to slow down Spencer and Fiorelli. But everything seemed to be going Hudson City's way. By halftime, the Hornets had a twelve-point lead.

"They might as well play with six or seven guys," Spencer said. "They can't stop us."

"There's still a long way to go," Coach Davis said. "Stick to our game. Hammer it inside; run when you have the chance. But think *defense*. Do not let them go on a run and get themselves back in this game."

Jared grabbed a towel and wiped his face and neck. He'd played every minute of the first half and was glad to have a rest. He'd probably played his best half of the season, grabbing a ton of rebounds, making nearly all of his shots, and not picking up a single foul. Everything was working today.

Fiorelli grabbed Jared's arm as they left the locker room for the second half. "See, my man? No pressure. Just excitement. We use that to our advantage. Am I right?"

"Absolutely," Jared said. "Let's keep it rolling."

And they did. South Bergen made a couple of short runs, getting the lead down to eight points in the fourth quarter. But the Hudson City players kept their poise. Jared finished with 24 points and the Hornets eased into the championship game.

"One more," Fiorelli said as the players swarmed into the locker room. "Hudson City. Basketball champions. Nobody thought they'd be hearing that a few weeks ago."

The Night Before

J ared stood in the kitchen and looked out at the driveway. The night was cold, but he needed to burn off some energy, to dribble for a few minutes at least and shoot some layups. All day long he'd been thinking about tomorrow night's championship game. Palisades had defeated Memorial in the second semifinal. Of course, Palisades had handled Hudson City the previous week.

"What's up, Jared?" Mom asked.

"Nothing," he said. "Just think I'll go out and shoot."

"This late? It's freezing."

"I know. But I need to blow off some steam."

"Why don't you play your guitar?"

"Not the same," he answered. "I need something physical."

"I see. Tomorrow's a big day, huh?"

"Giant."

Jared took the ball and headed outside. He dribbled in toward the basket and pivoted, turning his back to the hoop. He feinted left, then swerved and laid the ball off the backboard.

That would be the key. Get the ball inside and overpower the Palisades' center. Then stop him on the other end and get that fast break going.

Jared wanted to win the championship at least as much for his teammates as for himself. They'd come a long way, overcoming so many rough spots. Now, on the brink of the title game, he was more nervous than he'd ever been.

So much could happen. Palisades could shut down Hudson City's fast break the way they had last time. Jared could go cold and miss some crucial shots. He might even lose his temper again.

No, he wouldn't let that happen. He backed in toward the basket, dribbling the ball and working against an imaginary defender. He gave a quick juke to his right, then pivoted left and lofted a soft little jumper into the basket.

That was how it would go. Tough and focused. Physical but clean. Smart, hard basketball. That much was certain.

All or Nothing

J ared stared at the back of the seat in front of him on the bus ride to Palisades. They'd routed this team once but got pounded the second time. What would happen tonight?

"We'll run 'em ragged," said Fiorelli. Jason wasn't chattering as usual, but he kept making comments like that, trying to start a conversation. Jared would just nod and say, "Yeah." He could taste the meal he'd eaten right after school—a chicken parmigiana TV dinner. It was a spicy blob sitting in his stomach.

"We'll get the outside shots falling so they can't

double up on you, then hammer that ball inside," Fiorelli said.

Jared nodded again and glanced out the window. His breath made a steamy fog on the glass.

"I just wish we would get there and get started," he said. "The wait before the game is the toughest thing in sports."

The Palisades cheerleaders were on the court when Hudson City emerged from the locker room, and the pep band was blaring away. Banners hung on the walls above the bleachers on both sides of the court: "Rip Hudson City!" and "Palisades Rules."

Jared's parents and many others had made the trip to the game, but the spectators were at least 90 percent for Palisades. There was even some booing as Hudson City began warming up.

Spencer called the starters over and they huddled at the free-throw line. "We love this, don't we?" he said. "We love shutting people up."

"That's our mission," Fiorelli said. "The worse

they try to make it for us, the better we play."

"No intimidation," said Willie Shaw, who rarely said anything in the huddles.

"Championship game," said Ryan Grimes. "Everything we've worked for."

The other players all looked at Jared, who swallowed hard as the sour taste of tomato sauce came up. He stared at the floor for a few seconds, then lifted his head. "Five of us," he finally said. "A team. Nobody beats us when we play like a team."

"Amen," said Fiorelli. "Let's remember that."

Palisades came out fired up, showing much more energy than the subdued but patient Hornets. The point guard—Leon Johnson—had a hot hand early on. "Neon!" came the cry from the crowd every time he hit a shot.

Jared got a couple of rebounds, but Palisades hustled back to thwart the fast break each time. So Spencer bided his time, passing off to Fiorelli and the others and calling for the ball right back if a shot didn't open up. Eventually, the good shots came, and Hudson City kept pace. Fiorelli and Shaw each had a pair of baskets, and Spencer hit a three-pointer.

"Not bad," said Coach Davis after one quarter. Palisades led by two, but Hudson City hadn't gotten into any kind of groove yet. Jared hadn't scored and the Hornets hadn't run. "Look for the opportunities," Coach said. "Stay patient."

Opportunities, Jared thought. He motioned to Spencer as they walked onto the court. "Start driving to the hoop," he said. "I'll set the screen."

Jared had been thwarted by Palisades' big center in the first quarter, unable to get free. The Hornets needed to open things up.

Hudson City had the ball to start the second quarter. As Spencer dribbled near the top of the key, Jared struggled to get open under the basket. His bigger opponent stuck to him tightly. Jared took a quick sidestep, then made two quick strides to the side of the free-throw line. Spencer drove hard, slicing past Jared, who stood his ground as Leon Johnson crashed into him. Spencer shot past and went in unguarded for a layup.

"Nice job," Spencer said as they ran back to their defensive end of the court. "Keep mixing it up like that. They'll fold."

Johnson answered with a driving layup of his own, shooting the ball just over Jared's outstretched fingers.

Back on offense, Jared again moved to the foul line. This time, Spencer passed off to him, then darted toward the basket. Jared slipped him the ball on a nice give-and-go, and Spencer again made an easy layup.

"We're picking them apart," Spencer said a few minutes later during a time-out. Hudson City had taken a two-point lead, and Palisades seemed confused and sloppy on defense. Jared's screens and passes had led to two more baskets.

By halftime the lead was up to four. Jared hadn't scored and he had two fouls, but who cared? This was the championship game. They were leading.

"It's right there," Fiorelli said in the locker room. "It's like, one hour from now we'll be jumping up and down and screaming after we win this thing. Not 'Neon. Neon. Neon.' Try 'Spencer, Willie, Jared!' We just keep on playing our game, whatever way it comes down. If we need to nail the threes, we do it. If we need to hammer it inside, we do it. Whatever it takes. We do it."

Jared quickly peeled an orange and wolfed it down. His stomach had settled as soon as the game began, and now he was hungry and thirsty. He took several swallows of Gatorade and wiped his face with a towel.

"Let's run," he said, looking Spencer squarely in the eyes. "We get that fast break going and we can put these guys away."

But it was Palisades that went on the run as the third quarter began. They had brought in their backup center, who was smaller but quicker. Neon Johnson hit a layup and Palisades' other guard made a nice baseline jumper to tie the game at 28 apiece. The crowd went wild.

"No problem," Spencer said to Jared as he dribbled up the court. "You and me again. Let's go."

Jared moved to the basket, then hustled out to

set a screen for Spencer. Spence drove hard, using the screen, but the Palisades' center moved off Jared and picked up Spencer instead. Jared rolled toward the basket, and Spencer sent a bounce pass into his path. Jared hauled it in on the run and made his first shot of the game.

"Lots of options there," Spencer said as they ran back. "Keep picking them apart. You and me."

But Palisades kept up its hot shooting and gradually built a small lead. Then Spencer scored off another give-and-go from Jared, and Jared scored again on a feed from Willie. The teams entered the fourth quarter all tied up.

"Suck it up now!" Spencer urged his teammates in the huddle. "One more quarter. It's all or nothing."

Jared set a hard screen for Spencer on the Hornets' first possession, but was whistled for a foul. Palisades brought the ball downcourt and Johnson drove into the lane, forcing Jared to cover him. Johnson and Jared both left their feet, with the shooter twisting and getting off a shot as Jared tried desperately to block it.

Again came the whistle. Jared's second foul in a matter of seconds. Johnson went to the free-throw line. Fiorelli came over and gripped Jared's arm. "That's four on you," he said.

"I know," Jared said, spitting out the words and shaking out of Fiorelli's grip. "Two bad calls."

"Think!" Fiorelli whispered. "We can't have you foul out."

Jared shook his head in disgust and glared at the referee who'd made the call. Johnson made the first free throw, but the second one bounced off the back of the rim. Jared felt a new surge of energy and leaped higher than he even thought he could, grabbing the ball and coming down with his elbows out and his shoulders tensed.

"Right here!" yelled Spencer, and Jared made a hard pass to his teammate. Then Jared raced up the court, even with Spencer. The pass came to Jared, who immediately fired a pass to Fiorelli, well ahead of the others. Fiorelli took the ball straight to the hoop, and Hudson City had a one-point lead.

"Way to run!" Spencer yelled.

"All day!" said Jared.

Palisades came right back aggressively, with Johnson nailing a three-point shot from the top of the key. Again came the chant of "Neon! Neon!"

Jared took the ball out of bounds and carefully passed it to Spencer. "Let's shut them up!" he said.

Spencer nodded and gave a small smile. "It's coming to you," he said.

Spencer was true to his word. Jared took the ball just below the foul line and worked his way toward the basket, backing up his defender, who was all over him. Jared's shot was good, and he drew a foul besides. He made that shot, too, regaining a one-point advantage.

I'm taking over now, Jared told himself. *Both ends of the court.*

But Johnson owned at least one end. Despite Spencer's gritty defensive effort, Johnson hit another three-pointer, then added a driving jumper after a steal from Spencer in the backcourt. Palisades suddenly had a four-point lead. About three and a half minutes remained.

The Palisades fans stood and cheered as Hudson City took a time-out. Leon Johnson pumped his fist and pointed at the scoreboard. That team was fired up.

Spencer stared at the ceiling as the Hornets huddled up around Coach Davis. "He's killing us," Coach said, nearly shouting to be heard above the cheering and the pep band. "Let's go to a double-team. Willie, step out and help Spencer on Johnson. Nobody else is shooting, and Jared will control the inside. We've got plenty of time, but there's no tomorrow."

Jared grabbed Spencer's jersey above the number and put his face right up to his teammate's. "You okay?" he asked.

"No problem," Spencer mumbled, his eyes wide and angry. "Let's do it."

Jared overpowered his man for another layup, but Palisades came right back at them. Johnson drove to the free-throw line and looked to shoot, but Willie and Spencer had him covered. Johnson found the open man in the corner, and Jared bolted out to stop him. But that left the center wide open underneath, and all it took was a bounce pass for an easy layup. The lead was back to four.

Fiorelli made a basket, but Palisades came back with a pair of free throws after Ryan Grimes's foul. Jared connected on a leaning jump shot, but Johnson answered after eluding both Spencer and Willie.

Two minutes remained. Spencer dribbled slowly upcourt, catching his breath. Johnson waited at midcourt, ready to play aggressive defense. The spectators in the stands were shouting.

Jared stepped out near the foul line and waved for the ball. Spencer's pass was soft and high, but it didn't have much force. A Palisades forward stepped out and got his hand on the ball, and there was a wild scramble on the floor. Jared took a chance and ran to the basket, and the risky move paid off. Fiorelli got to the ball and sent an overhand pass to Jared, who made the easy layup.

"Press!" shouted Spencer, and the Hudson City players picked up their opponents in the backcourt. The ball went to Johnson, who easily broke the press by himself, darting upcourt and eluding Spencer and Willie.

Jared came charging up behind Johnson and cut him off as he drove into the lane. Jared planted his feet and took Johnson's full momentum, getting knocked backward and landing on his butt.

Jared closed his eyes as the whistle blew. *Not a fifth foul,* he hoped.

Not this time. The referee signaled for an offensive foul. Spencer grabbed Jared's hand and hauled him to his feet. "You're the man!" he said.

Hudson City had the ball and new life. The deficit was only two points, and Jared had a one-and-one free-throw opportunity.

Jared met Johnson's eyes as he stepped to the line. Johnson nodded and gave a half smile of recognition. There was an MVP trophy waiting for one of them at the end of this game.

Jared took the ball and bounced it twice, staring at the rim. He let out his breath and lofted the ball, watching the satisfying ripple of the net as the shot found its target.

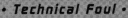

Same routine on the second shot. Two bounces. An exhale. A swish.

The game was tied.

"Don't press!" yelled Spencer. The Hudson City players ran downcourt and set up their defense, with Spencer waiting at the top of the key for Johnson.

Finally Johnson missed a shot, taking a long jumper that barely grazed the rim. Jared got the rebound and passed quickly to Spencer, then sprinted toward the opposite basket.

Johnson ran alongside Jared, determined not to let him get an easy bucket. But Jared had the size advantage, and Spencer got him the ball. Jared drove all the way to the hoop with Johnson all over him, then found Fiorelli wide open in the corner. Jason dribbled in and Johnson darted out to meet him. That gave Fiorelli an easy opening to pass back to Jared, who laid the ball off the backboard and in.

Palisades called time-out. Hudson City had fought back and taken the lead. Eighteen seconds remained.

"Spencer—you know who's shooting," Coach Davis said. "You give him an open shot, he'll nail it. I want five guys thinking nothing but defense out there. This thing is seconds away from reality."

"Let's go!" the team shouted as they broke the huddle.

"Used to be *you* telling Coach what to do," Jared said as they headed onto the court.

"He learned from the best," Spencer said, grinning.

Johnson dribbled up and surveyed the court. The Hudson City players were in a tight zone, except for Spencer, who was all over Johnson. He could drive the lane to try to tie the game, or he could work for an open three-pointer to win it.

Johnson passed the ball inside, then drifted toward the top of the key, calling for it back. Jared stepped out to meet the forward with the ball, closing off the lane as Fiorelli and Spencer hustled over to help.

The forward had no shot, but Johnson was open.

"Spencer!" Jared shouted as the ball flew out to Johnson.

Spencer darted toward Johnson, who dribbled once and shot. The ball arced toward the hoop. Jared turned to get ready for the rebound. The ball hit the back of the rim and rolled out, and Jared was there to grab it. He was immediately fouled.

Jared took a deep breath. Six seconds remained. If he made these two free throws, the game was theirs.

Johnson was standing with his hands on his hips, staring at the basket as Jared walked past him.

Jared made the first free throw. The best Palisades could hope for now was for Jared to miss and for Johnson to hit a long three-pointer. The spectators were stamping their feet and screaming for Jared to miss.

Jared dribbled twice and set his focus on the rim. The shot was true. Hudson City had a four-point lead.

"No fouls!" Spencer shouted as they ran back on defense.

Johnson shot from midcourt but the ball banged off the backboard. Hudson City had won the title!

Jared shut his eyes and made two fists. The crowd had been groaning, but now they were cheering. Hudson City had earned their respect. Fiorelli and Spencer and the others joined Jared on the court, thumping each other and shouting.

Spencer grabbed Jared's arm and pulled him close. "You're the man!" he shouted.

"Nah," said Jared, shaking his head and smiling. "No heroes, remember? The team. That's what this is about."

"We're the *men*," Fiorelli said, his face right in Jared's. He pointed at Jared, then Spencer, then Coach Davis. "You! You! You!" he said to each of them.

Jared could only laugh.

***

Tough Competition

The guy seated next to Manny on the basketball court inside the track had his eyes shut, nodding slowly to the rhythm of the music from his headphones. His shirt said NORTH JERSEY STRIDERS. Other runners were pacing the floor or stretching, all looking intense.

The gymnasium at Fairleigh Dickinson University wasn't quite as large as the Armory, but Manny was even more nervous for this meet. This wasn't a relay meet; there were no teammates to help carry the load. In a few minutes Manny would be out there for the 800-meter race with nine opponents.

He checked his racing shoes—double-knotted with the laces tucked in—massaged his thigh, and took a deep breath. He knew nothing about the other racers, didn't recognize any of them from the meet at the Armory. This was primarily a New Jersey event.

"Eleven-twelve boys' 800. Step up."

Manny got to his feet and bounced in place a couple of times. He was warm and loose. They'd had time to jog a full mile before the meet and he'd been stretching ever since. The track was the same length as the Armory's—200 meters—but the turns were flat.

He stepped to the starting line. The runners on both sides of him were tall and leggy. Manny crossed himself and shut his eyes.

"Take your marks," said the official.

Manny leaned slightly forward and exhaled hard.

"Set."

He clenched his fists lightly and stared at the track.

The gun fired and Manny surged from the line, darting to the head of the pack to avoid the jostling as runners fought for position. Coaches and teammates were shouting, but Manny's focus was entirely on the track. He could hear the padding of nine pairs of feet just behind him.

Pace yourself, he told himself. *Hold the lead, but be smart about it. Long way to go.*

Manny's goal was 2:18, the time Serrano had run at the Armory the week before. Who knew what Serrano would do this week; he was probably racing at the Armory again. All the results of the Armory meets were posted on the Internet, so Manny could compare his progress with Serrano's and everybody else's.

"Thirty-three," came the call as Manny finished the first lap, still holding the lead. He needed to average under 35 seconds per lap to meet his goal for today. He felt strong.

Manny glanced behind him as he raced along the backstretch. Coach had told him never to do that, but he couldn't resist. Two runners were just off Manny's shoulder, but the rest of the field had fallen a few yards behind. These two seemed content to let Manny lead the way.

Each stride felt smooth but Manny could feel his shoulders beginning to tighten. He passed through the end of the second lap at 67 seconds.

Fast, he thought. *Got to keep this up.*

Coach had told him that the third lap was often the most important one in a four-lap race. The runners were getting tired from a quick start and were saving some energy for a finishing kick. A strong runner could put away the race with a solid third lap. But the temptation was to hold back a little.

Manny surged into the turn, testing his opponents to see if they'd stay with him. They did more than that. The North Jersey Strider runner went wide on the turn and moved into the lead.

Don't let him get away, Manny thought. *Stick with him.*

They pounded down the backstretch in a tight cluster, but the leader surged again coming off the second turn. Manny opened up his stride on the straightaway, pulling away from the third-place runner and turning it into a two-man race.

"1:43," came the cry as the bell sounded for the final lap. Manny quickly did the math; that lap had taken 36 seconds. They were slowing down. *So what!* Manny hollered inside his head. *It's a race! Forget about the time.*

Manny moved to the outside edge of the first lane and stuck within inches of the leader. Around the turn and into the backstretch, his aim was to stay with this guy.

Arms pumping furiously, they headed into the final turn, puffing and grunting as they began an all-out sprint. The leader moved out to the line between the first and second lanes, forcing Manny to go even wider if he wanted to get past.

Onto the straightaway, just fifty meters from the finish. Manny dug for everything he had left. Closer, closer, and suddenly he had the lead. Leaning forward with no air in his lungs, his throat burning and his arms feeling like cement. The finish line, the tape against his chest. He'd won it!

Manny got off the track and settled to his knees. He put his fingertips to his pounding forehead and shut his eyes, gasping for breath. He lowered his hands to the floor and crouched like that for a few seconds, waiting for his head to clear and his breathing to slow down to normal.

Suddenly he felt hands around his waist and was pulled gently to his feet. "Fantastic race," said Coach Alvaro. "Walk it off, buddy. Don't lie there in a heap."

Manny took a few slow steps and inhaled deeply. He looked up at the coach and gave a pained smile. "Caught that sucker," he said softly.

"You sure did," Coach said. "You're a tough little guy, Manny. There's no quit in you."

Manny looked up at the bleachers toward his teammates and family. He raised his fist when he locked eyes with his father, then turned to the coach.

"What was the time?" he asked.

"2:19. Pretty darned good." Coach smiled. "Serrano better watch out, huh?"

Manny gave a tight smile and nodded. He'd used every ounce of strength and speed he had in him. Where would he find even more?

RICH WALLACE

was a high school and college athlete and then a sportswriter before he began writing novels. He is the author of many critically acclaimed sports-themed novels, including *Wrestling Sturbridge, Shots on Goal,* and *Restless: A Ghost's Story.* Wallace lives with his wife and teenage sons in Honesdale, Pennsylvania.